Arthur's
Christmas Wish

Written and Illustrated by
SHARON L. WOODING

Atheneum   1986   New York

Atheneum
Macmillan Publishing Company
866 Third Avenue, New York, NY 10022

Type set at Linoprint Composition, New York City
Printed & bound in Hong Kong by the South China
Printing Company
Typography by Mary Ahern

10 9 8 7 6 5 4 3 2 1

Library of Congress Cataloging in Publication Data

Wooding, Sharon.
Arthur's Christmas wish.

SUMMARY: Arthur's fairy godfather grants him his
wish to play two pieces on the piano well, but what is
he to do when he is asked to play all the music for the
school Christmas pageant?
[1. Mice—Fiction. 2. Christmas—Fiction.
3. Piano—Fiction] I. Title.
PZ7.W86037Ar   1986   [E]   85-28690
ISBN 0-689-31211-3

For Stephen
Hilary
and
Anson

Arthur snuggled down into the big armchair by the window in the front parlor. The plump mouse was feeling lazy after his walk home from school...and very hungry. He popped another cheeseball in his mouth and champed on it noisily as he watched the snow fall on the pine tree in the garden.

"I love holidays..." Arthur mused, "...chocolate eggs at Easter, pumpkin pie at Thanksgiving...but Christmas is my favorite." He closed his eyes and thought about rich, dark, plum pudding topped with creamy white sauce...cookies, candies....

"Ahem."

Arthur came out of his dream and looked up. Standing before his chair was a most peculiar looking mouse, a scrawny fellow in a light blue nightgown, a pair of tiny spectacles resting on the end of his pointed nose. Two small wings stuck out through the gown, and a long, hooded cape flowed down his back.

Arthur blinked. "Who are you?"

"I'm your fairy godfather, Arthur."

"My what?" demanded Arthur, wiping his whiskers with one hand and holding a fresh cheeseball in the other.

"Your fairy godfather! I've come to grant you one holiday wish."

Arthur had never seen anyone so silly-looking in his entire life. Fairy godfather indeed! "Those are pretty realistic wings you're wearing," he said.

"They're the real thing, Arthur. Let's talk about your wish. Since Christmas is a time to bring happiness to others, you must use a Christmas wish to make someone else happy."

"A wish to help somebody else! I want one for myself," whined Arthur.

The fairy godfather didn't answer.

Arthur stuffed the cheeseball in his mouth and thought for a moment. He looked around the room and noticed his mother's old piano.

"I take piano lessons," he said, "but I'm not very good—no time to practice I guess."

The fairy godfather gave an understanding nod and glanced at the music for "Spinning Song" and "Minuet in G" gathering dust on the piano.

"It certainly would make my mother happy if I could play for her," Arthur added, thinking of the treats he'd get for playing well. "As a matter of fact, I've decided on a wish. I'd like to be able to play those two piano pieces—really well, mind you."

"Enough said, Arthur. Your wish is granted." And with that, the fairy godfather disappeared like smoke from a pipe.

The next two weeks were wonderful for Arthur. He didn't need to practice the piano. He just sat down occasionally to dash off "Minuet in G" or "Spinning Song," and his proud mother rewarded him with goodies. He became chubbier and lazier than ever.

However, when his mother arranged a small recital for some friends and Arthur learned that one friend's daughter, Roberta, was coming, he became sulky.

"I don't want Roberta here," he grumbled.

"You're alone too much, Arthur," his mother insisted. "It will be good for you to have a friend over."

While Arthur's mother positively beamed, Arthur scowled his way through the recital. As soon as he was finished, he scurried to his favorite armchair. To his dismay, Roberta followed him.

"Arthur," she exclaimed, "I had no idea you could play so well."

"Pretty good for an old fatty like me, eh?" he mumbled.

"What do you mean?"

Arthur peered at her from the corner of his eye. "You mean you don't remember that you called me 'Fatty'?"

"No—well maybe. But that was a year ago, Arthur. I'm much more polite now."

"But you said it and you meant it. You don't like me because I'm fat!"

"Well, Arthur..." Roberta sighed. "I'm sorry I called you 'Fatty' a year ago."

Arthur looked away.

"I just wanted to tell you that I love the way you play the piano. You're sensational! See you in school tomorrow."

He felt himself blush after Roberta left. "You're sensational!" rang through his head. He wished now that he hadn't been so unpleasant to her.

At school the next day, the teacher, prompted by Roberta, asked Arthur to play for the class. Everyone loved his music, and the applause filled the room for a long time. At recess, a group of his classmates came up to him.

"Hey, Arthur, where'd you learn to do that?" one of them asked.

Arthur beamed. "Lots of practice, I guess. Would you like to try it?"

"Well, I don't know," the mouse responded. "Mom says I have a tin ear."

"Come on," urged Arthur. "I'll help you play the left hand of 'Spinning Song' with me. It's easy."

Arthur walked home from school that day with three new friends.

The next day, Mrs. Nita Pettigrew, who ran the annual Christmas pageant, appeared at Arthur's door.

"I've come to see you, Arthur," said Mrs. Pettigrew, "because we have an emergency. The musical director of this year's pageant has suddenly been called out of town. The program is only two weeks away, and there's no one to play the piano. Arthur, I've heard you breeze through 'Spinning Song' and 'Minuet'—well, I feel you're the only mouse in town who can possibly learn the pageant music in two weeks."

Arthur froze. "You want me to play?" How could he admit that he knew only two pieces and that he knew those only because of some sort of magic? He had begun to feel good about himself and didn't want to lose his new friends, and he wanted his mother to be proud of him. So Arthur agreed to play. What was he going to do now?

That night Arthur couldn't sleep. Finally he got up and waddled down to the parlor. He closed the door, climbed up on the piano stool, and spun himself around a few times till he was high enough to reach the keys. Then he opened the songbook that Mrs. Pettigrew had given him. He stared at the page and thought about the leftover cheese in the pantry. All those notes crammed onto that first page looked very confusing! He tried to play the first few notes, but they sounded awful. Arthur put his head down on the piano and began to cry.

"Watch out or you'll get the keys wet."

Arthur looked up, startled. It was his fairy godfather. Arthur quickly straightened up and tried his best to look unconcerned.

"I don't suppose I could have one more wish," he mumbled, staring down at the rug.

"Try it, Arthur," said the fairy godfather, and then he vanished.

Arthur returned to his music. He got through the first page, slowly and with one hand. Then he tried both hands, again slowly. He played softly until after midnight. The magic was working! He went to bed.

The next morning he practiced before school. He played again when he got home from school and all weekend, too. By Monday he had learned the notes to all five Christmas songs in the pageant. He now had eleven days left to get the timing straight and to make it sound like real music.

The week before the program Arthur practiced harder than ever. He was even too busy to think about snacks.

"Are you all right, dear?" his mother finally asked one evening when she noticed that the cookie jar had remained full for four days.

"Fine," he shouted, not pausing, even for a moment, from "Deck the Halls."

On the night of the pageant, Arthur's playing was a bit rough around the edges, but the chorus drowned out some of the mistakes and, after all, what could one expect of a young mouse in just two weeks? Arthur was elated after his performance. Mrs. Pettigrew, his mother, and many friends all hugged and congratulated him. He blushed when Roberta said, "Sensational!" and kissed his cheek.

Then Arthur noticed a mouse standing by the stage, his wings discreetly hidden under his cape. Arthur excused himself and made his way in that direction, but when he got there his fairy godfather was gone. There was only a piece of notepaper on the floor. He picked it up and read,

I granted you ONE wish, Arthur, the first one. You did the rest yourself.

With love, your fairy godfather

Arthur thought of his weeks of work learning the pageant music. He thought of the night he had cried at the piano and of what his fairy godfather had said. He hadn't ever agreed to a second wish. All he had said was, "Try it, Arthur."

And Arthur had done just that. Now, as he turned to his friends, who still smiled and clapped, he realized the magic was his own.